Faraway Farm

For Ella Rose Kennedy and Teddy Traynor
I.W.

For Holly
A.A.

ORCHARD BOOKS
96 Leonard Street, London EC2A 4XD
Orchard Books Australia
32/45-51 Huntley Street, Alexandria, NSW 2015
ISBN 1 84362 436 2
First published in Great Britain in 2005
Text © Ian Whybrow 2005
Illustrations © Alex Ayliffe 2005
The right of Ian Whybrow to be identified as the author and
Alex Ayliffe to be identified as the illustrator of this work has been
asserted by them in accordance with the Copyright, Designs and Patents Act, 1988.
A CIP catalogue record for this book is available from the British Library.
1 3 5 7 9 10 8 6 4 2
Printed in Singapore

Faraway Farm

Ian Whybrow
Illustrated by Alex Ayliffe

ORCHARD BOOKS

Faraway Farm lies over the hill.

Show me the house and the barn and the mill.

Into the kitchen comes Farmer Flat.

Where's his mug and his dog and his little black cat?

Breakfast!
The children all want to be fed!

Find me some eggs and some milk and some bread.

Time to get ready for milking now.

Where's the stool and the pail and the pretty brown cow?

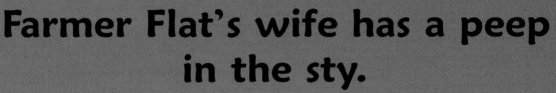

Farmer Flat's wife has a peep
in the sty.

She hears an "OINK! OINK!" – so what does she spy?

Here comes the tractor, the dogs run behind.

What other creatures and birds can you find?

Over the hill,
where the meadow is steep . . .

show me the rabbit and the lamb
and some sheep.

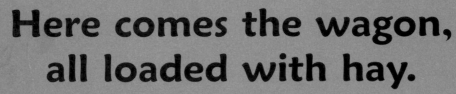

Here comes the wagon, all loaded with hay.

Who's in there riding,
all done for the day?

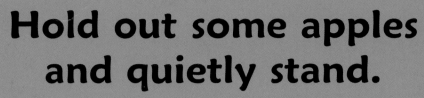

Hold out some apples
and quietly stand.

Who'll come and eat them from out of your hand?

Everyone's tired,
so out goes the light.

Who can we find to say, "Good night! Sleep tight!"